About the Book

The tomten is that small, silent creature who watches over the farm when everyone is asleep. Harald Wiberg first brought the tomten to life in two favorite picture books — *The Tomten* and *The Tomten and the Fox.*

Now Mr. Wiberg brings us CHRISTMAS AT THE TOMTEN'S FARM, which is not only a story of the tomten but also a classic picture of an old-fashioned Christmas on a Swedish farm.

Crisp, bold black-and-white drawings on a rich gray-green background and simple text combine to capture the clear, cold Swedish landscape and the warmth of Christmas as it is celebrated in Sweden.

Johan-Petter and his family live in a snug farmhouse surrounded by their barn, the henhouse and stable, the smokehouse, the storehouse, the animals — and the tomten who lives in their loft. How the family — and the tomten — observe Christmas Eve and the following two days — what they do, what they eat, the games they play, the spirit among good neighbors, and more—is all here in rich detail and enchanting pictures.

Harald Wiberg

Christmas at the Tomten's Farm

by WIBERG

E

Written and Illustrated by Harald Wiberg

Coward-McCann, Inc.   New York

Library of Congress Catalog Card Number: 68-15611
Printed in Sweden 1968 by AB Guto Tryck, Hbg

Far from the beaten track,
where the forest thins out and
the grazing lands begin, there
is a small farm called Kolartorp.
It lies between heaps of stones
and a tangle of fences.

Long ago, Johan-Petter was the
owner of this farm, and Kristin
was his wife. Their two children
were called Malin and Linus.
Grandmother Stava was also counted
as one of the family, although
she lived in a cottage nearby.

When they traveled, Johan-Petter and his family used a wagon or a carriage drawn by a horse. On special occasions they rode in a coach with springs. It was a black coach with decorations on the sides and on the seats, and the wheels had iron tires that rattled over the stony roads.

When they farmed, they used oxen
to draw the plough over the fields.
It was a simple wooden plough
which Johan-Petter had made himself, as he had made many things
on the farm.

Their storehouse was built on the
hill beyond the barn. It was
surrounded by tall, beautiful
junipers, but, of course, it was
not easy to reach in the winter,
when the snow was deep.

But don't think that Johan-Petter
and his family were the only ones
on the farm. The tomten was
there too. He watched over the
farm at night. No one would say

for sure that he had seen him,
but he was there. Everyone
knew that. He lived in the loft
above the cowshed.

The animals knew more about the
tomten than anyone else. The
wise old sow in the sty had seen
him many times at night. They
had long conversations.

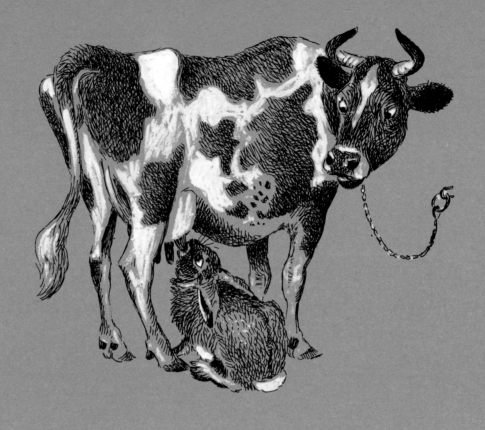

Everyone was happy to have the
tomten at the farm, but there were
other creatures they were not
happy to have there. The milk
hare, for instance. When the
cows went dry, people blamed the
milk hare. They hadn't seen him,
but still they said the milk
hare was milking the cows.

There were other evil spirits
that no one had seen. Farmers
believed, however, there were
ways to protect their animals
against these spirits. For one
thing, Johan-Petter hung a dead
owl over the door of the cowshed.
And in the spring, when he took
his cattle out for the first
time, Johan-Petter made them walk
over steel.

But now was not the time to think
of evil spirits. It was almost
Christmas. The autumn chores
were finished. The horse had
already had frost nails driven
into his shoes so he would be
ready for the icy roads of
winter.

The oxen, too, had been shod.
Each one had been taken into a
special shed, fitted into a sling,
then winched up from the floor.

Their stiff legs had been placed
on supports while crescent-
shaped iron shoes had been nailed
to the hoofs, one to each half.

Inside the house, preparations were also being made for Christmas. The spinning wheel was put away. The loom would soon be silenced. Kristin took the last length of cloth from it. Carefully she folded it, sprinkled it with lavender, and put it in the cupboard.

After many days of hard work with
his saw and ax, Johan-Petter had
the winter's supply of firewood
ready in the woodshed. Linus
had stacked more wood to dry in
the open shed.

The juniper beer was ready for
the Christmas table. The frost-
bitten berries had been picked
in the fall, and now the drink
was ready to be poured into
bottles and jugs.

The candles had all been made. Linus had helped dip the wicks into the melted tallow. Over and over he had dipped, until Kristin said the candle was thick enough. But sometimes Linus' candles did not turn out right.

December ninth, St. Anna's Day, was the day to start preparing the meat for Christmas. Early in the morning, while the stars were still bright, Karl-Johan, the village slaughterer, arrived at the farm. One of the pigs was fetched from the sty and led to the open space near the cowshed, where Karl-Johan was waiting. It was a happy time for the people on the farm, for now they would have fresh meat to eat, black pudding and sausage. Nobody asked what the pig thought about it.

Sausages, of course, meant hard work for Kristin. First she chopped up the meat with a pair of wooden meat choppers. Then she took well-cleaned animal intestines and used them for sausage skins. She slipped a skin over a cow's horn whose point had already been sawed off, and she pressed the meat in with her thumbs.

Some of the bacon was smoked in
the homemade smokehouse and
some of it, along with the sausage,
was salted in large oaken tubs.
Then the meat was taken up to the
storehouse on the hill.

Grandmother Stava helped with the
baking. So many different kinds
of bread for Christmas! Spiced
rye-meal bread, dipping bread, and
delicious cakes.

At last Christmas Eve came, and
with it came real Christmas weather. Snow was falling in large
flakes, gently and solemnly, as
Johan-Petter and Linus went across
the lake to fetch the Christmas tree.

Outside the kitchen window,
birds were flying backward
and forward. Bright red bull-
finches and black and yellow

great tits were celebrating
Christmas in the sheaf of wheat
that had been saved from the autumn
threshing especially for the birds.

When all the heavy work was finished, when the woodbox and the water pails were filled and the sheaf of corn in place, it was time for the Christmas bath.

Water was brought from the well in pails and warmed in caldrons on the fire. Everyone must be clean to celebrate Christmas.

The Christmas guests arrived—
Aunt Hannah with Grandmother,
Petrus, and fat Severin. It was
time for the first Christmas meal,
the dip in the pot. The kitchen
table was loaded high with food;
the broth in the pot was rich and
hot. Everyone ate enormous amounts.
They told jokes about neighbors
and talked about events in the
parish.

The cat lay beside a bowl of
cream before the fire, undisturbed
by the noise and bustle. He lay
with his belly up, which was supposed
to mean stormy weather.

That evening the children were given an orange to share, the only orange of the year. Then Kristin lit a Christmas torch. Everyone was so delighted with the torch, they didn't see the tomten at the window.

After a pleasant time around the
Christmas tree, they sat down at
the gate-legged table in the
kitchen and ate a supper of
dried fish and rice porridge.

Of course, all the animals must
be given especially good fodder
at Christmas. That evening,
Johan-Petter stayed with the
animals longer than usual.

He talked to them kindly
and quietly while he filled their
mangers. He wanted them to know
that it was Christmas.

The tomten knew that he, too,
would be remembered at Christmas.
He opened his squeaky door in the
loft, looked out at the moonlight,
muttered to himself, and climbed
over the threshold.

He walked silently, more lightly
than a cat. Still muttering to
himself, he walked between the
fences toward the barn and
outhouses.

"Good evening, Father," said the
owl sitting on a fence. The tomten
was startled. "Good evening, owl,
are you out tonight?" They stood
talking for a long time.

Below the steps leading to the
porch, Kristin was busy. She
was putting out a dish of rice
porridge for the tomten. It was
part of his annual salary from
the farmer and his family.

Inside, the family sat in the
bedroom. Father was reading
the story of the birth of
Christ. "And there were in
the same country shepherds abiding
in the field, keeping watch over
their flock by night." Kristin
wondered what it was like in the
holy country.

She wondered whether the fences were as well looked after as those at Kolartorp. Perhaps they were made of gold. And the people living there, where the Saviour was born, did they wear clothes of silk and velvet? Johan-Petter continued reading: "Ye shall find the babe wrapped in swaddling clothes, lying in a manger." Kristin saw the stall. It was her stall, hers and Johan-Petter's.

Then they went to bed, still
in a solemn mood. While they
were asleep, a little gray figure
stole along in the snow. It was
the tomten fetching his bowl of
rice.

In the light of a forked candle,
the tomten sat in a corner of the
loft among old clothes, mats and
tin cans and ate his rice. Olle,
the cat, and the mice kept
him company.

After the meal, while the mice
played their games, the tomten
went out the creaking door.
He went to the stable to see
his old friend, Blackie.

He also called on Rosa, the bell-cow. Although Rosa glared at him when he entered her crib, she was glad to see him. It was warm and comfortable there; the scent of hay filled the crib. Rosa mumbled something to the tomten. It must have been nice, because he was smiling as he went away.

Next the tomten took some food
to the sheep. He knew how rough
the old ram could be when he was
playful, so the tomten climbed
into the fodder rack, where he
felt safe.

After visiting the animals, the
tomten climbed up the ladder
into the hayloft. He peeked out
through a shutter in the wall.

There in the farmyard was the fox.
"I'd better see what he's up to,"
the tomten said as he hurried
outside.

There was a dangerous glint in the fox's eye. Although he knew quite well that on Christmas night there should be peace among the animals, he was staring at Olle, the cat, who sat in the middle of the farmyard.

The tomten was just in time to
rescue the cat. Then he scolded
the fox. With his head turned
aside and his ears laid back,
the fox appeared crestfallen.

Yes, yes, he promised to remem-
ber all that the tomten said,
but when the fox went away, there
was still a dangerous glint
in his eye.

The tomten shook his head as he
watched the fox go. Then he took
the cat into the cowshed.

In the light of the moon, the cat
got what he liked best of all—
a bowl of creamy milk.

Now the tomten went to the hens
to see how things were with them.

He asked the hens how they were
getting along, and the cock crowed
that everything was in order.
The hens were too sleepy to talk,
so the tomten wished them all a
Merry Christmas and crept away.

He went to the wagon shed. On
the way he met the cat and told
him to go indoors. "You never
can tell," he said. The tomten
had trouble with the tall doors
to the wagon shed, but at last
he managed to open them.

Inside the shed there was the "Sunday" coach, black and shining, and there were several wood sleighs meant mainly for the oxen. There, too, was the heavy clod crusher with its rollers of solid oak, and the huge charcoal basket in which charcoal was transported from the kiln to the ironworks.

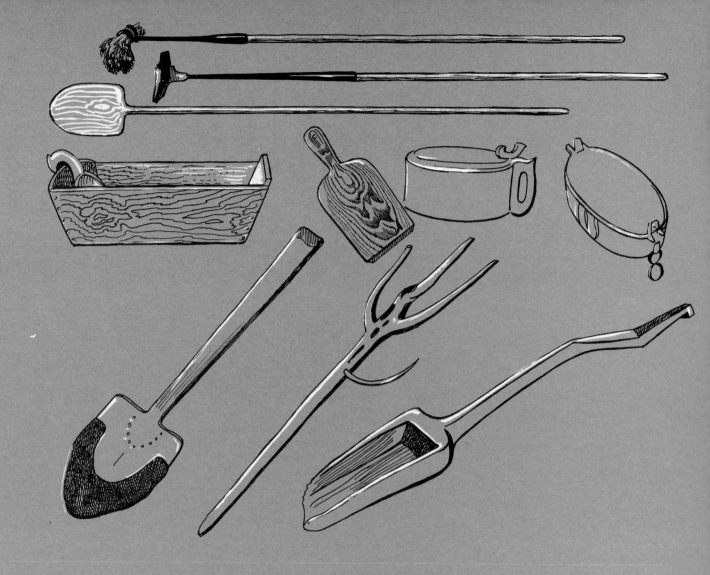

After the tomten had checked the
vehicles, he went to the building
where the tools and implements
were kept—the long oven brush,
the rake for raking charcoal

from the oven, the bread spade,
the beautiful food boxes,
the baking trough, the corn shovels.
And yes, there, too, was
the old pitchfork.

It was now three o'clock in the morning of Christmas Day. Everyone in the house was awake. While Kristin went into the kitchen to make breakfast, the children screwed up their eyes and blinked sleepily at the candle's light. Father scratched his back. They were not used to getting up so early.

It was pitch dark when Johan-Petter
went to the stable to feed the
horse. The cat followed, walking
in the circle of light at Johan-
Petter's feet; above, the stars
glittered in the sky.

When the horse had finished eating,
the family was ready to drive to
church. Johan-Petter pulled out
the finest sleigh and harnessed
the horse. Linus lighted the way
with a torch.

Away they went, over fields and into the woods, the bells of the horse jingling all the way. The light of the torch flashed among the trees, jumping from one tree trunk to another. Johan-Petter looked from side to side, while Kristin and the children crouched under the furs.

When they got to church, the horses
were placed in the church stables.
People gathered outside to talk
and gossip until it was time to
go in for the service.

Big, strong laborers, buxom farmers' wives, lean smallholders, and worn-out old women took their places according to rank and dignity. The organist played a Christmas hymn, and the clergyman read the story of the birth of Christ. He preached a long sermon, and at that early hour there were many who nodded in their pews.

After the service, there was hurry and bustle. The men harnessed their horses as fast as they could. They believed that the one who got home from church first would harvest the following year's crops before the others.

The solemnity of the morning service was gone now. The horses were driven as fast as they could run. The jangling of the bells was mixed with shouts and laughter. Pedestrians had to jump to the edge of the road.

The children went to bed for a few hours when they got home, but for Mother and Father, there was no time to rest.

After the wild race home, Blackie had to be cared for. And the cows had to be driven to water.

Cleaning out the cowshed was a dirty job, but it had to be done on Christmas Day as on all other days. But really, Johan-Petter enjoyed the work in the warm cowshed. He enjoyed making the animals happy with the clean straw under them.

The first day of Christmas was
a quiet time and seemed long to
the children. They were not
allowed to play outside. Instead,
they passed the time in front of
the fire, cracking nuts.

At twilight the quiet hours of
Christmas came to an end. The
cows had to be milked again,
whatever the day. The milk had
to be strained and poured into
cans and kept cold until the
next morning.

It was dark when the work in the
cowshed was finally finished.
Now the people on the farm could
spend the evening in peace.
But not the tomten.

He had work to do. He looked
through the window of the loft
and thought how happy he was
to help Kristin and Johan-Petter.

Kristin lit a forked candle on the table by the window. The flickering flames made the shadows in the room seem alive.

The light fell warmly on the everlasting flowers that stood between the double-glazed windows.

After dinner, which was eaten at the kitchen table, they all gathered around the Christmas tree with its lighted candles and decorations. In clear, high voices, the children sang Christmas carols, and their parents listened. Then the children received their Christmas gifts.

At the end of the evening, the
family went to bed. Now it was
the tomten's hour. And the hour
of the fox. He stole quietly
toward the farm.

Suddenly the tomten heard a well-known sound from the woods behind the storehouse. He smiled. "Those young people!" he said. It sounded like the hum of a huge swarm of mosquitoes. Instead, it was a long line of small tomtens, the ones who watched the charcoal kilns in the forest. Every Christmas they went from place to place, singing. And now they were running in a long line between fences and weather-bleached cottages on their way somewhere, no one knew where.

The young tomtens were far away
by the time the old tomten was
down from his loft. He went to
the meadow behind the woodshed.

He had some carrots under his
coat for a friend that always
came on Christmas night to visit
him. And there he was, as usual.

The tomten watched a wood mouse run about among last year's plants. If I were you, the tomten thought, I should hide somewhere. It is past midnight now, and you are an outlaw again. And the owl is out hunting.

The stars were still bright as
the tomten continued on his
rounds to the linen shed.
There was no one there now, but
when the linen was being dressed,
what a lot of noise and talk
there was! And it was not all
work, either. The tomten had
seen what the young people had
been up to at times, and he
smiled at the thought.

At the smithy one of the windows was open, and the tomten climbed in. Although it was a holiday, Johan-Petter had been there to mend a piece of broken harness. There was still a smell of burning wood, and there was charcoal glowing on the hearth.

Outside the smithy, the tomten
met Pelle, the gray house cat.
Together they looked up at the
Christmas sheaf set out for the
birds. It had received many
visitors; the ears were empty.
Well, the tomten thought, it
would be a shame to disappoint
any birds. He would have to
fetch a few handfuls of oats.

Suddenly the tomten remembered
his neighbor who lived under
the cowshed. It would never do for
good neighbors not to wish each

other a Merry Christmas. He
went to the stable to fetch a
lantern.

The tomten crept down under the
cowshed. The badger was a real
sleepyhead. All winter long he
stayed indoors under the cowshed.
All winter long he did nothing
but sleep.

He tried to talk to the badger.
"Merry Christmas, neighbor!"
he said. But the badger made
no reply. Soon the tomten
went away again.

And where was the fox all this time? The tomten was still suspicious of him. He went to the window of the poultry house. And sure enough, pretty soon, along came the fox, the deceitful rascal. But he didn't get far. The tomten drove him away while he was on the plank leading to the window.

It was almost daybreak now—
St. Stephen's Day, the second
day of Christmas. And it was
time for Johan-Petter to lead
the horse to water.

According to an old belief,
if a horse was watered before dawn
on St. Stephen's Day, he would be
protected from witchcraft.

Then Johan-Petter and Linus hitched
Blackie to the sleigh, and they
drove to the ironworks to deliver
the milk. Along narrow roads
they went, through many gates,
and over stony fields.

Three moose ran across the road
in front of the sleigh. Blackie
shied and would have bolted, but
Johan-Petter knew how to calm
him.

What a long way it was to the
ironworks, Linus thought. But
finally, all the milk was delivered.
The last can went to their friends'
big house by the road, and there
they were invited in to taste
the Christmas food.

The table in the best room had
been laid, according to custom,
ever since Christmas Eve. The
food was for visitors and would
stay there, covered with a white
cloth, right through Christmas.
Johan-Petter and Linus did not
need to be asked twice!

When they got home, the family
went to visit their neighbors
in the village. They walked in
a long line with Johan-Petter
at the head.

The children met other children
of the same age, and they all
talked about the Christmas
gifts they had received.

One of the boys had a toy flute.
He delighted everyone by making
weird and wonderful noises on it.

Later the games began. Snowballs
flew back and forth, hitting
first one and then another,
while shouts and laughter echoed
between the houses.

Together the young people made
a snowman out of huge snowballs.
They put a carrot in the middle
of a round face for a nose; they
used charcoal for the eyes and
teeth; and on top of the snowman's
head, they placed an ancient hat.

Meanwhile, inside, the women were in one room, gossiping and drinking coffee from saucers, and the men were in another room. Already they had taken their cake, one piece of each of the seven different kinds. What they could not eat, they wrapped in handkerchiefs to take home.

In the best room, where the lighted Christmas tree stood, the men and oldest boys played games of strength—tug of war, arm press, and raising masts. Cheered by the onlookers, the men pulled, pushed, and threw each other to the floor.

Wrestling was one of the most popular games. The men grappled with each other until their faces were as red as cockscombs and their joints creaked. As the evening progressed, the company became jollier and livelier— and noisier.

Then someone sat down at the organ
and began playing Christmas carols.
The tallow candles smoked and
flickered as with true Christmas
feeling, they sang together.

They kept on singing as they danced around the Christmas tree. But it was getting dark outside now and time to bring the evening to a close. They all said they would have to meet again soon. They thanked the host and hostess and set out for home.

Outside, the wind had been blowing
the snow into all kinds of fantastic
shapes. On the way home, the
children saw figures that reminded
them of strange animals pictured
in their schoolbooks.

When they got home, Kristin made a
fire. She and Johan-Petter sat
down and talked over the events
of the day, but the children stayed

outside. They made a snow lantern
in the yard and lit a tallow
candle inside it. How beautifully
it shone in the winter evening!

While Kristin prepared supper, Johan-Petter finished the work in the cowshed and stable. He filled the manger and saw to it that the stalls were dry and covered with new straw. Last of all, he led Blackie out for a drink of water.

Just before going to bed, Johan-Petter put the cat out. In the yard he stopped and looked about. Everything was peaceful and in order. He thought of the tomten and all the work he did secretly for the farm. Johan-Petter sent a Christmas thought to the loft over the cowshed. Then he looked up at the starry sky.

There everything seemed peaceful and in order, too. Johan-Petter turned back to the house. The second day of Christmas had co[me] to an end.